Violet and Victor write
the Most Fabulous Fairy Tale

Written by **Alice Kuipers**

Illustrated by **Bethanie Deeney Murguia**

Ⓛ Ⓑ

LITTLE, BROWN AND COMPANY
NEW YORK   BOSTON

I'm Violet Small and I'm six minutes older than my twin brother. I love writing and I'm a great storyteller. I want to write the most fabulous fairy tale in the history of fairy tales.

My name is Victor Small, but I am BIG.
I'm working on my Animals from Australia project.
In Australia—

Shh. I have a great idea
for my fairy tale.

Violet was born in a castle—

You were born in a hospital.

ENCHANTED
FOREST

WINGED
CREATURES

Ahem.

Princess Violet was
born in a gleaming castle
in Fairy Tale Kingdom.

BEANSTALKS

HOUSE OF SWEETS

TOWER

PUMPKIN PATCH

TO THE CASTLE

ENCHANTED FOREST

Fairy Tale Kingdom is a marvelous place. Princess Violet writes fairy tales about glass slippers and peas under mattresses and talking frogs.

Talking frogs don't exist.
In Australia there are *real* amazing animals, like
koalas and cockatoos and quokkas and kangaroos—

What's a quokka?

It's a short-tailed wallaby that eats—

Oh, never mind!

Fairy Tale Kingdom is filled with fairy-tale creatures. Talking frogs and swan princesses and multicolored unicorns and fire-breathing dragons—

and koalas and cockatoos and quokkas and kangaroos and—

It's *my* story.

I want a turn.

One terrible day in Fairy Tale Kingdom, a wicked witch invaded Violet's castle.

Victor!

The witch cried, "Witches are always wicked in stories!" So she banned fairy tales.

Stop!

She locked up all the creatures—

Why?

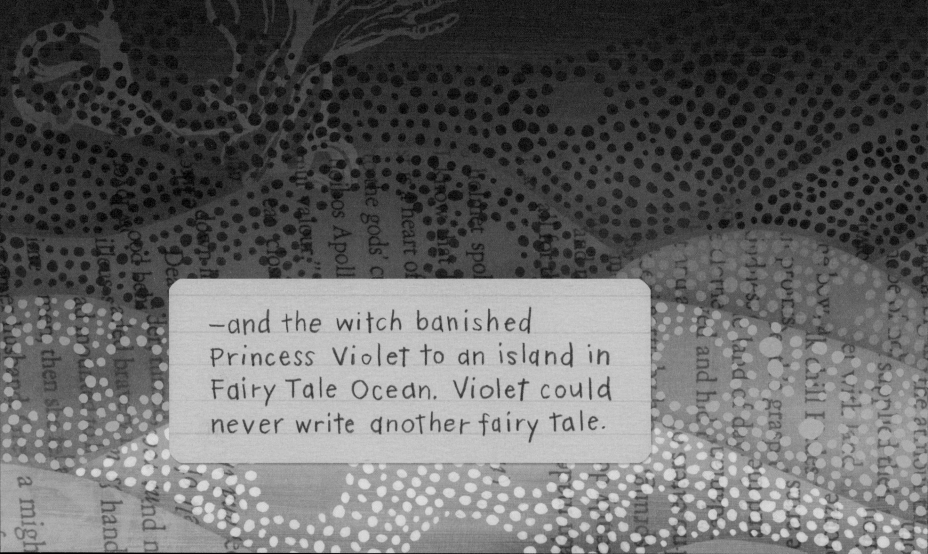

—and the witch banished Princess Violet to an island in Fairy Tale Ocean. Violet could never write another fairy tale.

It's my turn now!

Straightaway, Violet went to work on a plan to escape the island. She built a boat out of sticks and leaves—

But it was full of holes, so it sank.

She begged a passing
mermaid to help—

But the mermaid was too busy fishing for oysters.

So... Princess Violet summoned Prince Victor and his dragon!

Wait. I'm not in this fairy tale.

Of course you are.
You're my twin.

Well, dragons don't exist.
How about a cockatoo?

HERE BE DRAGONS

Violet and Victor climbed onto the back of Prince Victor's cockatoo. They flew over Fairy Tale Ocean. They landed secretly in the castle.

SERPENT SHALLOWS

DRAGON'S LAIR

MERMAID
BAY

That's not what happened!

They found the witch
and locked her up—

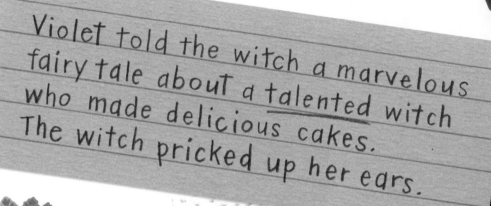

Violet told the witch a marvelous fairy tale about a <u>talented</u> witch who made delicious cakes. The witch pricked up her ears.

Violet told a brilliant fairy tale about a <u>happy</u> witch who loved Australian animals. The witch smiled.

Violet told the best-ever fairy
tale about a generous witch
who shared her delicious
cakes with all the Australian
animals. The witch giggled.
Now the witch loved fairy tales!

The talented, happy, generous witch released all the creatures. She shared the castle with Violet and Victor.

ENCHANTED
FOREST

Violet wrote the witch the most
fabulous book of fairy tales.
Everyone lived happily ever after.

Especially the quokkas.

WINGED
CREATURES

Especially the
multicolored unicorns.
Now shh, let's read.

For Yann, with love
—A. K.

For Ana and Audrey, thank you for reminding
me to believe in unicorns and dragons
—B. D. M.